THE SHY LITTLE KITTEN

by **Cathleen Schurr**

illustrated by **Gustaf Tenggren**

A GOLDEN BOOK • NEW YORK

Golden Books Publishing Company, Inc., New York, New York 10106

 Library of Congress Catalog Card Number: 97-71581 ISBN: 0-307-16141-2
First Little Golden Storybook Edition 1997 A MCMXCVIII

Way up in the hayloft of an old red barn lived a mother cat and her new baby kittens. There were five bold and frisky little roly-poly black and white kittens, and *one* little striped kitten who was very, very shy.

One day, the five bold little roly-poly black and white kittens and the one little roly-poly striped kitten who was very, very shy all sat down and washed their faces and paws with

busy little red tongues. They smoothed down their soft baby fur and stroked their whiskers and followed their mother down the ladder from the hayloft—jump, jump, jump!

Then off they marched, straight out of the cool, dark barn, into the warm sunshine. How soft the grass felt under their paws! The five bold and frisky little kittens rolled over in the grass and kicked up their heels with joy.

But the shy little striped kitten just stood off by herself at the very end of the line.

That was how she happened to see the earth push up in a little mound right in front of her. Then—*pop!*—up came a pointed little nose. The nose belonged to a chubby mole.

"Good morning!" said the mole, as friendly

as you please. "Won't you come for a walk with me?"

"Oh," said the shy little kitten. She looked shyly over her shoulder.

But the mother cat and her five bold and frisky kittens had disappeared from sight.

So the shy little kitten went walking with the chubby mole. Soon they met a speckled frog sitting near the pond.

"My, what big eyes he has!" whispered the shy little kitten. But the frog had sharp ears, too.

He chuckled. "My mouth is much bigger. Look!" And the frog opened his great cave of a mouth.

The mole and the kitten laughed and laughed until their sides ached.

When the kitten stopped laughing and looked around, the frog had vanished. On the pond, ripples spread out in great silver circles.

"I really should be getting back to my mother and the others," said the shy little kitten, "but I don't know where to find them."

"I'll show you," said a strange voice. And out of the bushes bounded a shaggy black puppy.

"Oh, thank you," said the shy kitten. "Good-bye, mole."

So off they went together, the shy kitten and the shaggy puppy dog. The little kitten, of course, kept her eyes shyly on the ground.

But the shaggy puppy stopped to bark, "Woof, woof," at a red squirrel in a tree. He was full of mischief.

"Chee, chee, chee," the squirrel chattered back. And she dropped a hickory nut right on the puppy's nose. She was very brave.

"Wow, wow, wow," barked the mischievous puppy, and off they went toward the farm.

Soon they came bounding out of the woods, and there before them stretched the farmyard.

"Here we are," said the shaggy puppy dog.

So down the hillside they raced, across the bridge above the brook, and straight on into the farmyard.

In the middle of the farmyard was the mother cat with her five bold and frisky little black and white kittens. In a flash, the mother cat was beside her shy kitten, licking her all over with a warm red tongue.

"Where have you been?" she cried. "We're all ready to start on a picnic."

The picnic was for all the farmyard animals. There were seeds for the chickens, water bugs for the ducks, and carrots and cabbages for the rabbits. There were flies for the frog, and there was a trough of mash for the pig.

Yum, yum, yum! How good it all was!

After they had finished eating, everyone was just beginning to feel comfortable and drowsy, when suddenly the frog jumped straight into the air, eyes almost popping out of his head.

"Help! Run!" he cried.

The frog made a leap for the brook.

Everyone scrambled after him and tumbled into the water.

"What is it?" asked the shy little kitten.

"A bee!" groaned the frog. "I bit a bee!"

Then they saw that one side of his mouth was puffed up like a green balloon.

Everybody laughed. They couldn't help it. Even the frog laughed. They all looked so funny as they climbed out of the brook.

The shy little kitten stood off to one side. She felt so good that she turned a backward somersault, right there in the long meadow grass. "This is the best day ever," said the shy little kitten.